CUDDLES *for* MOMMY

by Ruby Brown

illustrated by
Tina Macnaughton

little bee books

Little Owl wanted to give Mommy Owl a cuddle, but she couldn't decide what kind of cuddle to give her mom.

There was the cuddle you gave when you said good morning.

"But it's past morning, Little Owl," said Mommy Owl,
"and we've already had our good-morning cuddle."

Little Owl thought some more.

There was the cuddle you gave when you said goodbye. Mommy gave those cuddles when she dropped Little Owl off at school in the morning.

"Are you going somewhere, Little Owl?" asked Mommy Owl.

"Um, no," said Little Owl.

"What about the cuddle I give you when I'm sorry?" said Little Owl, thinking about the time she broke her glasses.

"Have you done something wrong, Little Owl, or made a mistake?" asked Mommy Owl.

"No," said Little Owl.
"At least I don't think so."

"I know!" said Little Owl. "You cuddle me when I'm scared, especially if I've had a bad dream."

"But what are you scared of now?" asked Mommy Owl.

"Nothing, actually," said Little Owl.

After a while Little Owl said, "I always give you a cuddle to say thank you. Like when you've bought me a new book."

"You can give me one of those cuddles later," said Mommy Owl, "because I thought we'd go to the bookstore this afternoon."

"Yay!" said Little Owl.

Little Owl thought
some more.

What other reasons
were there to give
her mommy a cuddle?

"We cuddle when we're really happy," said Little Owl, "like the time I won the art competition."

But before Mommy Owl could answer, Little Owl said, "I'm happy right now, but not *excited* happy."

Little Owl

"And then there are the cuddles you give me when you're proud of me," said Little Owl.

Mommy Owl nodded. "I was VERY proud of you last week after your trumpet performance at the school concert."

"Or," said Little Owl, "when I'm sick, you ALWAYS give me a cuddle then. And that ALWAYS makes me feel better."

"That's true," said Mommy Owl, "but you're not sick right now, are you?"

"No," said Little Owl, "which is a good thing," she added.

"Maybe I could give you a good-night cuddle," said Little Owl hopefully. Then she frowned. "But I'm not ready to go to bed yet."

Suddenly Little Owl's eyes grew very big. She had a fantastic idea....

"I know what kind of cuddle I can give you RIGHT NOW, Mommy!" said Little Owl.

She wrapped her wings around Mommy Owl and squeezed tight.

"The Mommy Cuddle! Just because I love you!"

 little bee books

An imprint of Bonnier Publishing Group
853 Broadway, New York, New York 10003
Text copyright © 2015 by Chirpy Bird
Illustrations copyright © 2015 by Tina Macnaughton
This little bee books edition, 2016.
Manufactured in China APO 1115
First Edition 2 4 6 8 10 9 7 5 3 1
Library of Congress Cataloging-in-Publication Data
is available upon request.
ISBN 978-1-4998-0203-0

littlebeebooks.com
bonnierpublishing.com